CAPIN MACK

and the
Giant Squid

John Lomas-Bullivant

Chief Engineer Samson

Giant Squid

Captain Mack

Tracy Trickster

The Mayor

Marty Meddler

Grabby Crabby

Peter Patent

Yolanda Yummy

Dr Kwack

Daisy Digger

To Mum and Dad With Love – JLB

First published 2010 by Walker Books Ltd
87 Vauxhall Walk, London SE11 5HJ

2 4 6 8 10 9 7 5 3 1

Text copyright © 2010 John Lomas-Bullivant
Illustrations copyright © 2010 Walker Books Ltd

Design and illustrations by Dynamo Ltd

The right of John Lomas-Bullivant to be identified as author of this work has been asserted by him in accordance with the Copyright, Designs and Patents Act 1988

This book has been typeset in Kronica Regular

Printed and bound in China

British Library Cataloguing in Publication Data:
a catalogue record for this book is available from the British Library

ISBN 978-1-4063-2360-3

www.walker.co.uk

www.captainmack.co.uk

The submarine has crashed and is stuck between some rocks.

Captain Mack
needs to act fast
to save the crew
who are still inside.

But what's this? Some kind of sea creature?

Suffering submarines! It's a giant squid. Watch out, Captain Mack!

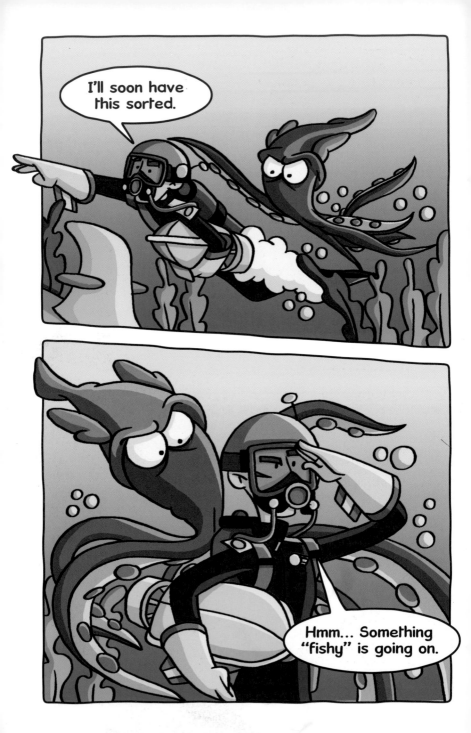

Captain Mack sets off on another dangerous mission.

But what kind of monster could have come from outer space?

Elsewhere...

Ooh! Look! What do you think they are, Grabby?

I don't know, Yolanda. But they look very scary.

They look exactly like Space Monster footprints...

Arghh! It's a disaster! CALL CAPTAIN MACK!

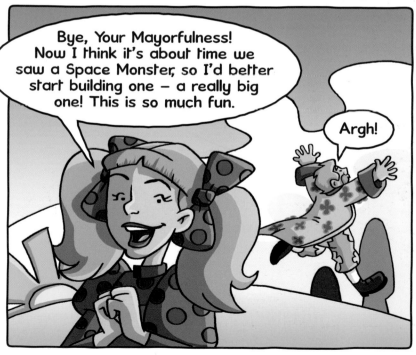

SNIP!

SCRITCH!

SCRATCH!

STICK!

GLUE!

A little while later...

Tracy, Tracy! You've got to hide. There's a Space Monster in Sunshine City.

I know! It's asleep in front of the Town Hall. Tee, hee, hee!

Not that one, Tracy. That's just the BABY! Its MOTHER has come to Sunshine City and she's FOUR times as big!

Arghhh!! Help! Captain Mack!

TO BE CONTINUED...

Nov 2010

June 2011

Nov 2011

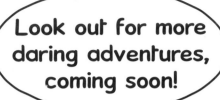

Look out for more daring adventures, coming soon!

For more fun stuff visit:
www.captainmack.co.uk